Driving

Madness

Michelle Krabinz

Michelle Krabinz was born in Cologne in 1994 and has been drawn towards the art of writing since her early years of puberty. Even though she wrote a lot of short stories and fairy tales, she never thought about becoming a professional writer until she was in her early twenties.

Since then she has discovered not only a love for all kinds of art, but also the wish to share her numerous stories and fantastic worlds with other people.

"Driving Madness" is her first novel which is written in English and was partly written during her two months travel through the United Kingdom. But even though she has fallen in love with the Scottish landscape, the story is placed in a small town in Germany – so don't be surprised that people are driving on the right side of the road.

Driving

Madness

Michelle Krabinz

Die Deutsche Nationalbibliothek verzeichnet diese
Publikation in der Deutschen Nationalbibliografie;
detaillierte bibliografische Daten sind im Internet über
http://dnb.dnb.de
abrufbar.

Herstellung und Verlag:
BoD – Books on Demand, Norderstedt
ISBN: 978-3-7460-6353-9

Driving Madness

For Jörg and Sabine,

who always made me feel safe

when I got into a car

New girl in town

"Did you already hear about her?"

"About whom?"

I turned away from my car to face the guy who was currently trying to fix the engine.

"About this freak they let out of the nut house?"

"There are many freaks getting in and out of madhouses everyday – and even more walking around, not being caught. Which one are you talking about?"

"The girl who went nuts in one of her driving lessons and killed her own driving instructor."

Sam cast a meaningful look into my direction and my eyes flickered to the sign on the top of my school car. *Just because I am a driving instructor doesn't mean that every lunatic in the world will be coming for me ...*

"So what? Has she declared that I will be next or why are you telling me this like it is the most important thing in the world?"

Sam eyed me with a disapproving look. I could guess that he had hoped for a bit more concern on my part.

"She hasn't 'declared' anything yet. They just let her out a week ago. But I've heard some rumours that she and her lone mother will be moving into our town."

My eyebrows showed a little bit of astonishment and Sam acknowledged it with an approving nod.

"Yes, you've heard right. It's nothing official of course, but a friend of mine knows the mayor of the town where she was locked up and it's been said that he gave our own mayor a little warning about her."

I contracted my brows and tried to cope with this new information. *If it's true ... Yeah, what then? They won't just let her drive like that, right? She might never be allowed to touch the steering wheel of a car ever again ...*

"Well, thanks for the notice," I finally answered and turned my concentration back on the engine of my car.

In the back of my head my brain still tried to understand what this information might mean for me and the driving school of my father. He had been a driving instructor as long as I could remember and I bet that he had already heard about this, too. *Maybe he just didn't tell me, because it's not a fact yet. Why should he bother to worry me with uncertainties ...?*

The part of my brain that was watching Sam noticed that he had now finished his work and was signalling me to start the engine, so that he might see if everything was back to normal again.

When he was satisfied that everything worked, I followed him into the little shop and tried to ignore the curiosity that was building up in my mind. When I had paid and waved goodbye, I drove home as quickly as I could without crossing any speed limits. The black Merc of my father was standing in the garage as always and I repeatedly told myself that everything was just as normal as ever. Still my heartbeat refused to calm down and I opened the front door with the brooding feeling of awakening disaster.

"Dad? Are you home?"

The call was unnecessary – *where else would he be while his car is here?* – but I still sighed in relief as I heard his familiar high voice sounding out of the living room.

"I'm here, son. Did you stop by at Sam's place like I told you?"

"Yes, I did," I answered while I took off my jacket and boots and finally stepped into the living room. "He repaired it within a few minutes. Just a loose cable in the engine."

"I see."

The grey haired head turned towards me as I stepped into the room and the light blue eyes gave me a scrutinizing look. I had always hated it when he watched me like this – up to my twentieth birthday I felt guilty at all times, even if I wasn't – but now I looked into the old eyes with gratitude and actually felt happy to witness this attitude of his once more.

Like I am going to die any second … Absolutely stupid!

"Is everything all right, son? You look a bit worried."

Observing as always. But today I loved him for it.

"Actually, I am a bit confused about a matter Sam told me about."

I didn't have to say anything else. Thorben Vogel was the best informed person when it came to any car incidents around town and certainly the mayor himself had warned him about the potential thread.

"I guess Sam told you about this lunatic that is running free again – the one killing innocent driving instructors for sport."

"Yap. He didn't put it like this, but that's the one I'm concerned about. Who told you?"

"Mayor Jenkins."

"I thought so."

"He wanted to give all the driving schools a little heads-up, so that we might decide for ourselves if we want to take the risk of teaching such a lunatic or not."

My eyes bulged in horror.

"No way! They are going to let her drive again?"

"Yes, if anyone is crazy enough to accept her at their school."

"But how could they approve to let someone like her behind a wheel? This is insane!"

"Probably. According to her doctors she is back to normal again. Her psychiatrist has given an official report in which he states that she has been completely cured for one year and didn't have any relapse since then."

"But this is … I don't know. I'm not sure if she should be trusted with such a high responsibility if there is even the slightest chance for a relapse."

"I totally agree with you, son. But it's what the doctors said. As long as nobody accepts her at a driving school we might still have a chance to keep our streets safe. I've already spoken to a few of them and nobody really wants to have her. So I think we can relax for now."

"Uh-huh."

I wasn't quite convinced, but there was nothing I could do, so I just sat down on one of the leather armchairs and stared into oblivion, trying to get a clear head.

"Why did she kill her driving instructor in the first place?" I finally asked and turned to look into the testing old face.

"I'm not quite sure. It's been on the news a few years ago, but all you can find now is rubbish. Nothing of real significance. The only thing I know from the report of her psychiatrist is, that she stated to have been attacked by aliens and thus crashed the car into a tree on the side of the road."

"And only her driving instructor died?"

"Yes. It's actually not quite clear why he wasn't able to prevent the accident. He died on the spot and she herself endured some serious injuries."

"Serves her right," I mumbled under my breath.

"And there was a third person in the car."

"Really? Sam didn't mention that …"

"It's not a well-known fact. I'm not sure why they kept it from the public, but there was a driving examiner in the car, too. He suffered severe injuries. I haven't heard anything else about him."

"You mean the incident took place during her driving test?"

"Yes. The examiner is supposed to have said that everything was going pretty well and that she seemed to be in real control over the car. The accident happened so suddenly that even he didn't see it coming."

I furrowed my brow and tried to make sense of all this, but my brain couldn't get a clear picture. There were too many missing pieces in this puzzle. *Why did this accident happen? Did her brain just snap and she really thought they were attacked by aliens? Or did she kill her driving instructor on purpose? But why would she do that? And why during her driving test if it was going so well? She might have walked out of there with a driving license and no blood on her hands – what made her change her mind?*

The choice to kill

Her head was focused in the utmost concentration and her face didn't give away a single thought. She had had enough time to practice the skill of a poker face and now was the time to prove it.

The gaze of the driving examiner burned holes into the back of her head, but she resisted the urge to look at him in the rear-vision mirror. Instead she kept her eyes fixed on the street and traffic.

The presence of the examiner was by far not the worst, but he was the one who might erase all her hopes and plans of the last few weeks. If it hadn't been for him, she might have wiped the ugly smile of the face of her driving instructor fifteen minutes ago!

"Please turn left in a hundred metres, we want to get to the motorway."

The voice of the examiner was friendly and warm. He seemed to be a very nice guy and had smiled ever since she had managed to reverse into the parking space without effort. Now, thirty minutes after they had started the driving test, he seemed to be in high spirits and obviously thought, that he would get out of this car, congratulating her on a successful test. He didn't know yet that he might not even see the end of the day …

She turned to the left with ease and accelerated quickly to get on the motorway without a problem. Everything went perfectly – but her plan was falling apart with every minute that passed and she still hadn't come up with an alternative.

Luckily her brain picked up the speed too and her thoughts were racing down the motorway, far ahead from their car and this troublesome situation. Then it hit her. She knew that route. They had driven along this exact street a million times and she was sure about what was about to come. Within seconds the new plan unfolded within her mind and when the driving examiner told her, that they wanted to get off the motorway at the next exit, a faint smile found its way onto her face. The B-road was the perfect chance!

She even knew which tree she would pick. The only thing she had to consider now was who was going to die and who might stand a chance to live on. Her driving instructor had been destined to lose his life as soon as he had gotten into the car. She would have preferred to die, too, because what would follow a survival wasn't exactly her favourite way of living. It was either jail or the madhouse – both not really promising for a young girl in her early twenties. But if she killed herself, the chance of the driving examiner's survival wasn't very high and he seemed to be a very nice person. Probably not completely innocent – who lived to fulfil that expectation? – but harmless and nice enough to deserve a chance to live.

So she would have to find a way to crash the car in a way that guaranteed the death of her driving instructor and leave all the other people in the car as unharmed as possible.

I can do it! I have prepared for this moment long enough – I have to succeed! No other options. It's either die or live for the examiner, but this devil beside me will go straight to hell!

On the edge of sanity

Since the day Sam had told me about this lunatic, she hadn't left my head and I was always a little edgy when I drove to our driving school to give a lesson. Luckily my father was still fit enough to do most of it and the woman he had hired for the office work was doing a pretty good job, too. So I mostly concentrated on the motorcycle lessons – because my father had never really gotten the hang of bikes – and sometimes filled in if he had to give a theory class.

That was the case today and I was doing a night drive with a guy nearly my own age who looked like he was going to fall asleep any time soon.

"We're nearly there. Just one more corner and you can see the driving school. See?"

The guy – I had forgotten his name as soon as the engine was started – nodded nervously and we drove onto the courtyard like a slug on its deathbed. When he finally stopped and turned off the engine, we both sighed in relief and I forced a smile on my face.

"That wasn't so bad. It's always more difficult in the dark. You'll get used to it."

"All right. Thanks George. I'm really sorry for the last bit, I just wasn't able to fall asleep last night and my eyes were burning like hell …"

"Yeah, that can happen. Just stay sharp for the next lessons. My father is a bit stricter about dozing off during a drive."

"Yes, sorry. It won't happen again."

"Sure."

We stepped out of the car and he mumbled a few more thankful words before he turned to his scooter and I waved him goodbye. When he was finally gone, I drove the car into the garage and checked the interior of the school, before I went home myself. The speed of the motorcycle helped to clean my head and I felt wide awake, flashing through the night like a shadow. *I really don't get why father doesn't like it! It's awesome to feel the wind lashing around you and being one with the machine. Far more direct than a car. Maybe that's what women love about horse riding …*

When I got home, the Merc was already there and I smelled the aroma of cooking dinner as I stepped into the house.

"Hey dad. I'm home."

I heard muffled voices from the kitchen and stopped dead, the helmet still in my hand and about to turn on the light in the hallway.

"Dad?"

The voices went silent and I stealthily put down my helmet and started to sneak up to the kitchen door.

"George, is that you?"

The sound of my dad's voice nearly made me jump and I just caught the umbrella that had been leaning on the wall I bumped into.

"Yes, it's me."

"Oh, good. Dinner is nearly ready. And we've got a few visitors. I hope you don't mind."

I finally straightened up and turned around the corner – only to find the kitchen crowded with every single owner of a driving school in the whole town. *All right, it's a small town and so there aren't as many people as there might be in a big city. But four men, including my father, gathered in a kitchen — it's a picture every housewife would laugh at.*

"Hello George," I was greeted happily by everybody and shook hands with all of them before I turned to my father.

"Am I allowed to know the cause for this surprise?"

"Well, we were just discussing the matter of Ruth Kunze and because we weren't finished, I invited everyone to stay for dinner."

"Um … Ruth who?"

"Ruth Kunze. It's the lunatic we've talked about."

"Oh. All right. So she has a name now …"

"Yes, the mayor has officially announced that she will be moving into our town."

"Really? I didn't hear anything about it …"

"Well, he just told all the driving teachers and owners of driving schools. I'm sure he knew that I would tell you about it right away, so he didn't bother sending two messages for us."

"I see. So she's coming for us."

I looked into earnest old faces and knew that this wasn't a matter for jokes.

"This is serious, George. She might be a real thread … "

"I know, I know. I'm sorry. I was one of the first who said that she shouldn't be allowed to drive anymore, so everybody calm down."

The furrowed brows brightened up a bit and everybody started to move again.

"Well, as I was just saying," Bernard began to speak and the conversation continued like I had never interrupted it.

I only listened with half an ear while I took off my protective clothes and quickly ran my fingers through my tangled brown curls. With a glance into the mirror in the hall I decided that I was presentable enough to join the others and went back to the kitchen – just when everyone started to move into the living room to sit down around the big table.

"If we just tell the mayor that none of us want to have that girl, she and her mother might change their minds and move to another city," Bernard was just saying and everybody nodded in approval.

"Oh, so they're already here?" I asked astonished and the nodding continued.

"Yes, they moved in today. That's why it was made official now. We don't know yet if her mother really plans to get her into driving school any time soon, but we thought it might be best if we unite now and act while we still have a chance."

"Sounds like a war's coming," I mumbled under my breath and tried to keep my face solemn to match those of the others.

The discussion about our next move continued while we ate dinner and didn't cease until a quarter to midnight. After the reminder that we all had to work early in the morning, everyone started to get going and finally the house was silent again – at least for two seconds.

"You didn't say much tonight. What's the matter? I thought you were on our side."

My father made it sound like I had committed some kind of treason with my silence and I tried my best to remind me that it was just his love for me that made him ask so many questions.

"I'm fine, just a little tired. And everybody else was saying a lot, so I don't think you might have missed anything I could have said. That's all."

"I see. Well, you should go to bed then. Get some rest. We'll have a busy weekend."

"Really?"

"Of course. We've got to write a petition to our mayor and if this Ruth should show up at any of our schools, we've got to warn each other."

"Um ... All right. I'll go to bed then. Good night."

"Good night, son."

I dragged myself up into the bathroom and felt like my head was about to explode with information. All those endless discussions about our strategy and safety measures had made me really tired and I just wanted to fall into my bed and sleep – just sleep until all of the madness was over. *Maybe that's how this Ruth felt before her brain snapped – too much pressure from all sides, expectations and people who had high hopes for her. She was probably a perfectly normal girl who wasn't able to cope with everybody's hopes and dreams.*

I lay in my bed and stared into the darkness around me. *Am I getting mad, too? Will my head snap if everyone continues to make such a fuss about it?*

Beyond the border

The trunk of the tree was only a split second away and she could see the horror in the face of her driving instructor as he realised there was nothing he could do. His feet slammed the brake, but nothing happened. He was about to turn his head to her and their eyes met for one final moment of satisfaction. She felt the triumphant grin on her face and saw the shock as he started to realise who had decided his fate – then the side of the car hit the tree and everything went black.

She didn't even hear the crumbling metal or the sound of shattering glass. Just silent nothingness and then an unpleasant ring in her ear. It was a high-pitched sound which erased all other sounds. Then the pain kicked in. Sharp pain, pinching her like burning needles. And she opened her eyes again. Everything was blurred and didn't make any sense. She could see lights flashing in and out of sight. Blue lights, white lights – too many lights! They were blinding her and somehow the ringing in her ears grew more intense.

It threatened to burst her head, but then it stopped and instead there was sound. The sound of sirens, many voices calling and shouting, hurried footsteps. Everything was too much. She wanted to put her hands over her ears, but she couldn't move. First, she stared down at her hands in disbelief, not understanding the combination of limbs and technique she was seeing. Then a sound louder than the others turned her attention towards the back of the car. In the cracked glass of the rear-view mirror she saw a man getting dragged out of the car by two people with uniforms. Were those firemen? Her head couldn't answer the question, the pain was too loud. So she concentrated on the man who was covered in blood and now put onto a stretcher. Then her head remembered something and she turned it towards the seat on her right. Her eyes couldn't cope with the image and she turned away quickly – only creating new pain and regretting it instantly. From then on she kept her head still, half turned and watched the picture on her right from the corner of her eye.

She was pretty sure that there had been a seat once and even a person sitting in it, but now neither seat nor man were recognisable anymore. They had turned into some confusing mess of blood, flesh, glass and metal and her brain wasn't up for the challenge to put it all together.

She just sat there and observed while she listened to the voices outside the vehicle. When one of them sounded right next to her left, she dared to move her head again and stared into the face of an unknown man.

"Hello Miss. Are you all right? Can you hear me?"

She just looked at him, not fully understanding the meaning of his words or knowing how to respond. The man now waved for another one to help him and they somehow managed to lift her out of the car.

"Just stay still, Miss. Help is on its way."

'Help' came in the form of another stretcher and she was carefully put onto it and hurriedly carried away. Then everything went black again and her mind was no more...

Secret doubts

The weekend passed by in a blur and I tried to stay reasonable and sane. Everybody around me seemed to have gone mad over the matter and I couldn't help feeling, like I was the one imprisoned in a madhouse.

After the mayor had received our letter of concerns and answered, that nobody would force anyone to accept Ruth Kunze at their school, some of the old men were pleased enough to carry on like usual. My father was one of them and so our daily routine returned. He went to the driving school every day and I worked at my half-time job in the local bookshop. We didn't have any pupils for motorcycle right now, so I only had to step in if another dork should decide to take his night drive on a Monday or Thursday night. This didn't happen most of the time, because Charlotte kept an eye on the matter and had promised me to spare me if she could. So it was just a coincidence that I showed up on exactly this evening.

It was Friday and the bookshop had closed early, because of a long weekend. I was about to drive home when I remembered that I had promised Charlotte to stop by this week. With a sigh, I turned my motorcycle around and sped down the road through the fading light of day. It was round about six o'clock when I reached the driving school and Charlotte was the only one left.

"Father already went home?" I asked after wishing her a good evening.

"Evening, George. Yes, the last driving lesson was at 4 pm so he went home to prepare dinner or something like that."

"Always the good betty. At least since mom died. I can tell you that it took a while until he managed not to set the kitchen on fire every time he turned on the stove."

Charlotte chuckled and turned her head towards the screen of her computer.

"I guess you didn't drop by to rail about your father. So let's see what we've got for you next week. Oh, what a surprise! Nothing at all."

She smiled at me and I gave her a thumbs up.

"Just like I prefer it. Thanks a lot, Charlotte. You're my guardian angel."

She blushed and hurriedly turned her head away. When her gaze fell outside the window, her smile dropped and her cheeks suddenly lost all the colour they had just displayed.

"What's the matter? Did you see a ghost?"

I turned my head, too and noticed a car sitting in the parking lot on the other side of the street. It wasn't familiar, but our town wasn't so small that I would know all the cars everyone kept.

"I don't see anything out of the usual ..." I started, but Charlotte kept gazing at the car with a face of horror.

"Do you know this car? Is it someone who is bothering you? A stalker?"

"No," she finally managed to answer, with a voice that was barely more than a whisper.

"It's the fact that I *don't* know the car."

"But you don't seriously mean to say that you know every car in town, right?"

She opened her mouth for an answer, but in that moment, I heard the opening door of said car and her lips formed a slim line of defence.

I turned once more and watched cautiously as two female figures made their way towards our door. Finally my body took over some of the tension that was radiating from Charlotte and I prepared myself for the worst case. Well, at least I thought about it, but I couldn't really decide what I would have to do if this was really Ruth Kunze with her mother who were approaching.

The doorbell rang when they stepped inside and I didn't take my eyes of them for one second.

"Good evening," Charlotte's feeble voice sounded to my left and I knew she was trying her best to keep up a poker face.

"Good evening," replied the older woman and smiled faintly at both of us.

My eyes stayed cold and so she quickly turned her full attention towards Charlotte, while the eyes of the younger female met mine without any sign of discomfort. Actually, there was no sign of any kind of emotion. Just two blank, green screens who continued to stare at me.

"How may I help you?" Charlotte asked politely and the older woman fought to keep the smile on her face.

"I would like to register my daughter for driving lessons."

I could feel the tension building up and cast a quick look into Charlotte's half frightened face. Her poker face was crumbling.

"And may I learn the name of your daughter?"

Her voice was starting to shake a little and the older woman didn't fail to notice.

"I am very sorry if you should have heard anything bad about my daughter. Her name is Ruth Kunze and I am her mother, Emilia Kunze."

Charlotte's face turned into a mask of ice. The head of the young female now turned to watch her instead of me.

"I am very sorry, Mrs. Kunze. But I have indeed heard things about your daughter and the owner of this driving school has decided to refuse to let Ruth join our school."

The face of Emilia turned desperate and I kept a close eye on the reaction of her daughter. Ruth stared motionless at Charlotte, without any sign of understanding or regret.

"Please, Mrs …?"

"Miss! Peach."

"Please, Miss Peach! We have asked in several driving schools already and you seem to be our last hope. I can absolutely understand your doubts, but doesn't everybody deserve a second chance? My daughter has endured so much since this incident and has shown real regret for what has happened. It wasn't really her fault altogether. So couldn't you just give it a try? Maybe for a few weeks, to see if there's a way for this to work out?"

The despair in Emilia's voice showed real compassion for her daughter and I tried to make out any kind of reaction in Ruth's face, but there was none.

"I am sorry, Mrs. Kunze, but this is not my decision. The owner of this driving school has set his mind. You'll have to come back on Tuesday if you want to speak to him personally. Beside that there is nothing I can do for you."

Emilia slouched her shoulders and turned to me in some kind of last attempt of hope.

"And you, Mister? Could you help us out?"

I shook my head, but the coolness in my eyes melted away in the presence of her desperation.

"I'm sorry, Mrs. Kunze. There is nothing I can do for you."

My reply seemed to have killed her last hopes and she turned away with a face of someone who accepts his defeat.

"All right. Thank you very much. We'll be back on Tuesday then. Good evening."

She turned for the door and was halfway out when her daughter finally started to move, too. Ruth walked slowly towards the open door, but just before she reached it, she turned her head one last time and looked at me for a second. Her eyes showed the hint of a hidden plea, then she was gone and the door closed with ringing bells.

"Gosh, this nearly scared me to death!" Charlotte exclaimed when the car with the two women was gone. "Did you see the face of that Ruth-girl? She looked like she was in a daze! Totally out of her mind, I tell you. To let someone like this behind a steering wheel would be a crime!"

I just nodded and tried to convince myself that I still believed in this, too. But this last second where she had looked at me had somehow pierced through my wall of defence and now I stood there, not knowing if I should brace myself or rather embrace another truth: The truth that Ruth Kunze might actually be back to normal and really deserved a second chance.

End of a world

Her body ached all over and she didn't dare to open her eyes. She'd rather stay in this comforting darkness than return to the world of voices, colours and madness. So she kept her eyes shut tight and tried to make out the source of the pain. It was ubiquitous and seemed to absorb all thoughts and feelings. It might have been overwhelming, but she was actually quite used to pain and so she managed to clear her head bit by bit. Pictures started to flash through her mind. Memories of fast flashes of light and colour, which didn't make any sense at first. But she didn't give up and the jigsaw puzzle in her brain started to put itself together piece by piece. The car. She had been in a car. The car of her driving school. And there had been two other people. She couldn't remember their names, but she clearly pictured their lifeless bodies, covered in blood. The one in the back must have been alive, because they transported him with an ambulance. But the other man, the one beside her, had definitely been dead. The first corpse she had ever seen in real life. The picture of his body, which hadn't made sense to her when she was sitting beside him, was getting clearer now and she could make out his smashed body: Blood everywhere, cuts and glass all over the skin, bones sticking out in places where they shouldn't be …

She shook her head and tried to ignore the feeling of sickness which started to build up inside her. This mass of flesh had once been her driving instructor – and she had killed him. Why had she killed him? Oh, yes. How could she have forgotten that?!? No, she would never be able to

26

forget what he had done to her. But now was not the moment for self-pity. She was alive and he was not. She didn't know if the other guy had survived, but even if he did, she would be arrested for murder and aggravated assault. Whatever had been before that accident, it would never be again. She was a killer now and she would have to bear the consequences of her actions. Or was there another way? Actually, it hadn't been her fault, her driving instructor was the one to blame for all this misery. If he wouldn't have been the devil that he was, nothing of this would have happened. Would anyone believe her? She didn't believe in justice anymore. So there would have to be a different solution, a way out of this hell of pain. The physical pain was endurable and would cease eventually, but the painful memories were burnt into her skull forever. How might she ever escape from her own head? This thought struck something inside her memory. An idea began to carve itself out of all the abyss and filled her with new hope. If she pretended to be insane, it might spare her the lifelong sentence in a prison. But she would have to be absolutely sure about it – no room left for mistakes.

She thought about this opportunity for a long time, while the bodily pain began to get stronger again. Maybe they were taking away her medicine to punish her for her crimes. Probably she even deserved it. Murder was a serious sin and wouldn't just be forgiven, that was for sure. But if she could convince the court and the doctors that she had gone mad, they might at least let her get off with just a few years in an asylum or something like that.

So she embraced this new personality of hers and began to forge out a plan for her hearing.

27

The power to forgive

"She really dared to come to my driving school?"

Father was nearly out of his mind when I told him about the incident at the dinner table and completely forgot to finish his meal.

"Yes. Her mother, Emilia Kunze, said that they had been to every driving school in the whole town already. Everybody turned them down, so she came to us."

"Unbelievable! How does she dare to force this devil upon us?!"

"She didn't look much like a devil actually. Both, I mean. They seemed quite normal. Mrs. Kunze was pretty desperate – it must be really important for her that her daughter gets a second chance."

"I don't care what this woman wants! This lunatic is not getting in my car and that's it. Good that you were there actually. Charlotte must be out of her mind right now. I bet she could use a vacation after this."

"Yes, she seemed to be a little scared."

"Understandable. And this girl, Ruth – what did she look like?"

"Um … Green eyes, brown hair – not like mine, a little lighter actually. It was rather short, I guess they shaved it off in the madhouse …"

"That's not what I meant, son."

"Oh. Sorry, I didn't get your question then."

"I was asking how she was? Did she look mad? Wild eyes or something?"

"Oh, I see. No. Her eyes were quite … calm. She was very quiet, didn't speak a word. But the way she looked at me in the end – it seemed like she really wanted to get another chance, too. Maybe it is her way of salvation or something: If she gets her driving lesson she will be freed of her sins. I don't know. Anyway, she seemed to be … normal, sort of."

"Uh-huh."

My father gave me another of his searching looks and finally turned his concentration back on his meal. We spent the rest of dinner in thoughtful silence and pondered over the question whether this Ruth might be trusted with the responsibility of driving a car again.

Maybe it would be possible to give her a limited license or something, so that she would only be allowed to drive in the presence of her mother. On one hand that might ensure that she won't cause another accident, on the other hand it might endanger her mother. But maybe we could give her driving lessons at least, so that she'd be able to get rid of her trauma or whatever it is … She wouldn't have to be let to drive alone at all. Maybe a few lessons would be enough to cure her, so that she might leave her bloody past behind her.

"You are really thinking that we should give her a chance, aren't you?"

As observant as ever, my father's eyes hadn't missed a single furrowed brow and he was giving me a very disapproving look – *like I am the madman now …*

"Well … I just thought that it might be possible to test her in some sort of way. She could go to a few theory classes and then we might see if we entrust her with our car. Only a few lessons at first, just so that we may see if it helps her condition. Maybe she will never get a license, but she might at least get a chance to find forgiveness or whatever she is seeking."

"I can tell you what this lunatic is seeking …"

"Her name's Ruth."

"Whatever. She is seeking another opportunity to kill, that's what she's after. Those mad people never really change. Their madness is just put to sleep by lots of meds and then she's let out into the world like a time bomb. She might be all quiet now, but the time will come when she seeks blood again and I don't want you or me sitting in the car with her if she does!"

I saw the worries in his light blue eyes and couldn't help appreciating his love and compassion. At the same time, my mind showed me the memory of Ruth's mother, who seemed so desperate to enable a normal life for her daughter.

"I understand your doubts, dad. I wouldn't want you to get harmed, but I am willing to believe that we may be safe from her. The madness has been cured, her doctors said so and she really didn't seem to be dangerous or insane. I bet she wishes to forget all those bad memories and maybe the only way to do so will be another driving lesson."

I could see in his old face that some part of him agreed with my argumentation, but the larger part still wouldn't give up on his worries and fears.

"This doesn't seem right to me. We have agreed with all driving schools that we wouldn't let her endanger our town and we should stick to that decision."

"Do you fear that the others would call us traitors?"

"No, I'm afraid that somebody might get hurt! And I definitely don't want it to be *you*!!"

The discussion seemed to be over, because he suddenly took his empty plate and went into the kitchen with a face of stone.

I guess I can't hope for any support there … At least not while everybody thinks that Ruth will murder all of us as soon as she gets into a car. I'll have to think of a way to prove that she isn't the lunatic they believe her to be. But how?

I decided that this would have to wait until Tuesday when Emilia and Ruth came back to our school to talk to my father. He would turn them down, I was sure of that, but it might give me a chance to speak to them afterwards. Maybe I could find a way to evaluate the degree of sanity that could be expected from Ruth.

The path of insanity

"Don't let him touch me! He's an alien, too!!!"

She screamed at the top of her lungs and felt like her body might burst open any second. The pressure of the tight arms that surrounded her and kept her in check, threatened to squeeze her to death, but the pain of her still wounded body helped to keep her rage burning. She continued to shout about the alien attack that was about to happen and tried to get away from the guy with the sedative injection as long as possible. Finally the strength of the adrenalin ceased a little and she couldn't keep up the fight for long. The sedative started to work instantly and the whole world wrapped itself up in cotton wool, until she wasn't able to see a clear picture anymore. Everything was blurry, even her thoughts, but one thing stood out as sharp as a razor: I am insane. This thought kept pulsating through her brain and helped her to focus on the act of insanity she was trying to perform.

Dull voices reached her cotton ears and she tried to put the words in her messed up head. She wasn't sure if she had understood them right and didn't really know if her answer left her mouth in the way that she intended it to do. But the judge – a blurry mass of black and white – nodded and turned towards a group of people on his left.

She gave up on following the events with her fuzzy vision and instead started to hum the national anthem. Why it had come to her mind she didn't know, but it fitted to the words in her head somehow: I am insane. I am ...

The court now started to move – or was it a trick of her eyes? – and slowly she realised that she was taken away. Where? She did not know. Why? She did not care. The whole world consisted of one simple sentence now: I am insane.

She followed the blurred figures that were taking her to some unknown place and lost track of time on the way out of the courtroom. When her senses started to sharpen again, she suddenly was in some kind of cell, wearing a straitjacket. Had she been imprisoned yet? Was this her sentence or would there be another hearing? Would they leave her like this? And had she managed to convince them of her madness?

The questions bubbled up inside her and seemed to consume her whole being. Time and space were falling apart around her. For the first time in her life she started to grasp the meaning of 'All things are relative'. It might have been minutes, days or years until the door to her cell opened up again and she was brought into the courtroom once more – this time wrapped up tightly in her straitjacket and closely watched by men in white gowns.

All the voices around her seemed to be a lot louder than before and hurt her dizzy head. When was the last time that she had drunk something?

She reminded herself to listen to the voice of the judge and this time she understood what he was saying. The court had decided that she wasn't in the condition to be judged normally. Instead of going to jail, she would spend the next ten years in a psychiatric facility, until the doctors decided that she was cured. She had to keep her face in check so that instead of relief, an emotionless mask clouded her eyes and locked out everything else.

Changing sides

Tuesday arrived with lots of grey clouds and a chilly wind that kept most people inside their houses. I myself didn't really want to get out of the warmth of my blankets as well, but father was already preparing breakfast and if I wanted to have a chance to meet Ruth and her mother before he had scared them away for good, I would have to hurry.

With a grumbling sigh I got under the shower and hurriedly went down for breakfast.

"Morning, dad."

"Good morning, son. I didn't know you were up yet. Don't you have the day off?"

"I do, but I wanted to accompany you to the driving school and see if Charlotte has managed to leave her world of fear. Otherwise you'll be in need of an office worker."

"True. Very thoughtful of you."

His blue eyes told me that he knew perfectly well why I was really going to join him, but he didn't mention the topic and I was grateful for the temporary peace.

We drove to the driving school with separate vehicles – I didn't want to stick around for too long if Charlotte was there and I had finished my job with Ruth – and so I reached it a few minutes earlier. Just when I had put my motorcycle into the garage, father turned onto the courtyard and soon afterwards another car appeared. I instantly recognised it and quickly went inside to warn Charlotte. When I entered, she greeted me with a smile, which instantly turned into a grimace as I told her who was about to visit us.

"Oh no! Not again."

"Don't worry. Father will handle it."

Relief spread over her face, just when the sound of the bell made our heads turn towards the door. It was father, soon followed by the two women. We all hardly fit into the little lobby and I tried not to stand in anybody's way – I didn't want to get caught in the cross fire.

"Good morning. You must be Mr. Vogel."

Ruth's mother instantly got to the point and explained to my father that she just wanted him to give her daughter a chance to prove his prejudices wrong.

"Please, Mr. Vogel. One driving lesson, just to see if it works out."

"I'm sorry, Mrs. Kunze. This is not an option. And that's my last word."

Father cast a critical look at Ruth – who met his eyes unafraid and emotionless as ever – and then turned to leave for the classroom.

"Goodbye."

His voice made it clear that there was no hope left and Emilia turned away with wet eyes.

"Thank you for your time. Goodbye."

She was out of the door before Ruth started to react at all and I wondered if the medication had had a permanent effect on her reaction time. I used the few seconds to give her a closer look and searched for any sign of abnormality. Her green eyes were as blank as always, but I couldn't help thinking that this just might be some kind of safeguard to protect herself from the hatred of the world around her. Her light brown hair didn't even reach her chin yet and was slightly curled, which gave it a natural look of wildness. Apart from that her whole posture and movement indicated nothing but shyness and calmness.

Then she slowly started to move her hands and I heard Charlottes frightened gasp. Next second I was beside Ruth's arm and ready to grasp it, but she wasn't holding a gun or any other weapon. Instead she put a packet of chocolate onto the desk and actually smiled at Charlotte – without so much as looking at me.

"I wanted to apologise for any inconvenience I might have caused you, Miss Peach. I am very sorry to have frightened you last time. That never has been my intention. Please accept my apology."

Charlotte just stared at her in disbelief until she finally remembered her manners and tried to force a smile onto her face.

"Thank you very much. I do accept your apology."

Ruth surprised us even more by returning the smile with something like real emotion in her eyes and then turned to nod into my direction, before she walked out of the door with a soft "Goodbye."

Charlotte and I stared after her and I nearly forgot why I had come here in the first place. When I did, I hurriedly ran out into the cold breeze and reached their car before Ruth had gotten into it.

"Excuse me. Mrs. Kunze, would you allow me a word with your daughter, please?"

Emilia looked at me, first puzzled and then with a glint of hope in her eyes.

"Of course. Would you like to get into the car? It's quite cold outside."

"That's true. If you wouldn't mind … It won't take long."

"Please have a seat, I'm in no hurry."

"Thank you."

I could feel Charlotte's look of horror on my back as I got into the car and sat down on the back seat beside Ruth. She ignored me at first until she had put on her seatbelt and then turned her eyes to me so suddenly that it nearly made me jump.

"So what did you want to talk about, Mister …?"

"Oh, I am sorry. I am George Vogel."

"Ruth Kunze."

We shook hands quickly and then she continued to stare at me with an intensity that even surpassed the searching glances of my father.

"Well … Um, may I call you Ruth?"

"Yes, of course."

"Thank you. Well, Ruth … I just would like to ask you a few questions. I am a driving teacher at this school and even though I may not surpass the decision of my father, I could possibly talk some sense into him. But for that you'll have to answer me truthfully and without holding back any information that might influence my decision. All right?"

"Yes."

"Great. Well, first I'd like to know why it is so important to you to have a driving lesson at all. I mean after all that happened it would be perfectly

37

understandable if you wouldn't want to get into a car ever again. So what do you expect to achieve by that?"

Ruth stared at me with careful curiosity and I couldn't see anything in her eyes that might have indicated a buried madness or some kind of time-bomb-insanity.

"I hope to forget the past and start all over again," she finally answered with a voice which didn't give away anything about her feelings concerning this topic. "I know that a man has died as a result of my actions and I can understand, that there are people who don't think, that I may deserve a second chance. But I have shown real regret and with the help of my doctors I was able to fight the bad parts of my mind which were responsible for this incident. So I would just like to resume life with the highest amount of normality that is possible."

"And driving a car would help you to do this?"

"I hope so. My psychiatrist and I agreed that it might help to let go of my trauma with the whole accident, so I just wanted to give it a try. If it doesn't work out for anyone, we might put an end to it immediately. All I ask for is a chance to try."

I quickly pondered about that information while I tried to read those mysterious green eyes in front of me – without any success. It was like she shielded her thoughts and emotions so that I was only able to see what she wanted to show.

"All right, this all sounds very reasonable. I would like to ask you another question though. Why did this accident happen in the first place?"

Out of the corner of my eyes I could see Emilia clutching her hands around the steering wheel and pressing her lips together like she was preparing for a crash herself. Ruth on the contrary stayed perfectly calm and answered as serene as before.

"The doctors explained it with a malfunction of my brain. We were driving down a country road when I suddenly saw a spaceship attacking the car in front of us. I didn't want to get shot by aliens, so I tried to turn around and we crashed into a tree. My psychiatrist explained to me that this was all an illusion of my brain and I know now that aliens and spaceships don't really exist. I haven't seen an alien in over a year and I am confident that something like this will never happen again."

I couldn't believe what I had just heard and tried my best not to show my confusion – with not as much success as Ruth had with her poker face. At least I didn't laugh out loud and told her that this was absolutely ridiculous and believing in aliens was something for children.

Well, she didn't do it on purpose, her brain created an illusion. It wasn't her fault.

"Have you watched a lot of science fiction movies in your past?"

"Quite a few, yes. And I loved those books as a kid. I always wanted to live in a spaceship. Or on another planet."

"And your doctors said that your brain works normally now?"

"Yes. They checked it lots of times and everything is perfectly all right."

"I see. So there is no medical objection against your mental health which might forbid you to drive a car alone?"

"Correct. And I wouldn't even be driving alone. You would be there, wouldn't you? You could watch over me and nothing bad could happen."

I was about to tell her that I actually didn't give regular driving lessons, but then I decided that this wasn't the right thing to say now. *Actually, it wouldn't be a 'regular' driving lesson, so why shouldn't I be the one to drive with her? Father definitely wouldn't do it ... In fact, nobody else will. Am I really her only chance? Shit! How am I going to persuade father??*

"If I am informed correctly, your driving instructor was with you in that car crash, right?"

For the first time, something like an emotion flashed through her eyes, but it was gone so fast that I couldn't really make out what it was.

"Yes, he was. He was the one who died."

"Oh. Yes, right. I'm sorry. But I just wondered: If he was there, why didn't he prevent the accident? Didn't he have some time to react?"

Ruth eyed me with real interest now and I couldn't help thinking that it actually helped her to talk about the whole thing.

"I don't know. I don't remember it very clearly. I was so distracted by the aliens – which weren't really there of course – and didn't notice anything else until I woke up in the crashed car. The police said that he might have tried to prevent the accident, but didn't have enough time, because we were too fast. A hundred kilometres per hour is pretty fast if you're suddenly racing sideways into the trees."

I tried my best not to imagine the situation too clearly and hurriedly changed the topic.

"Yes, well, thank you very much for your honesty. I can see why you would like to forget those past events and if a driving lesson really might be the key … Let's say I will try to talk to my father about this one more time."

Ruth just nodded while I could see Emilia beaming at me in the rear-vision mirror.

"Oh, thank you very much, Mr. Vogel. It would be a real help for us. Thank you."

"You're welcome. Well, have a good day then."

"Thanks, you too," Ruth said and turned her concentration out of the window.

"Thank you, Mr. Vogel. Shall we come back tomorrow then?"

"I think Thursday would be better. I'll need some time to discuss this with him."

"Yes, of course. Thursday then. Thank you."

I nodded once more and got out of the car. The icy wind had me shivering within seconds and I hurried back into the warm office of the driving school to reassure Charlotte that I was still alive and healthy.

Redemption

She had always had a blooming fantasy, but this was a whole new level. To convince all doctors and psychiatrists every day that she really believed in aliens was proving to be quite a challenge. Her head actually started to feel more confused and she feared that she might go insane after all.

Watching the other resident patients wasn't helpful to stay clear in the head either. There was one guy who believed he was the President of the United States of America and kept on babbling about building a giant wall.

She tried her best not to get in contact with any of the other patients and stayed on her own most of the time. The nights were even worse than the days: The darkness was full of noises creeping up on her and screams which resonated through the white corridors. There seemed to be only two colours in this madhouse: An impenetrable blackness – which filled her sleep with shadows and scary dreams – and the omnipresent white which was supposed to clean up their sinful souls. At least that was what one of the patients had told her on her first day in the madhouse.

How long she had been here now, she didn't know. Time was endless in this place of insanity and soon she lost track of things. Memories mixed themselves with present events and the picture of blood on her hands and broken bones kept haunting her wherever she went.

For the first few weeks she kept telling herself that she was glad about what she had done, but then came the first doubts and started to infect her thoughts with guilt and despair.

Even though the world might believe it had only been the fault of a mad brain, she had killed someone. She was a killer, a murderer. Would she be burning in hell already if she hadn't made it out alive? Was her driving instructor in hell? He definitely deserved it, but did she deserve it, too? Hadn't it been an act of kindness towards all those whom he had hurt?

The only thing she had wanted to do was to protect all the others from what had happened to her. But was that enough to justify her actions? Or would she have to atone for the sin she had committed?

Maybe those cruel dreams and frustrating months in the madhouse were her personal punishment – would her sins be washed away if she stayed long enough?

The battle of righteousness

"Are you out of your mind?!"

I had never seen my father so furious – at least not since schooldays were over and I had stopped to smoke weed.

"No, I'm not. I'm quite earnest about this actually and Ruth isn't out of her mind, too. She is a reasonable young girl who wants to forget the horrors of her past. Is this really so hard to understand?"

The blue eyes stared at me cold and disbelieving, while the thin mouth turned into a battle line of rage.

"This girl has killed somebody. She doesn't deserve a normal life, she has *taken a life* from somebody else! And she'll spend the rest of her life making up for that. That's what is called justice."

"No, this is called narrow-minded and unfair. Of course, she has done something terrible, but we aren't the ones to judge her for that. So we should try …"

"It is not our responsibility to help this girl! We have nothing to do with her and I would prefer it if that continued to be so."

"Why? She really regrets what has happened! And her doctors said that it might help her to get rid of her trauma! Isn't that something one should support? I bet she will be even less of a danger to our community if we give her a chance to move on and forget about the past."

"The best thing for our community would be if she just left town!"

I sighed and had to hold myself back from rolling my eyes at him.

"Why can't you just try to find a little bit of forgiveness and kindness for her? She hasn't attacked you personally and her doctors say that she is back to normal again. Why wouldn't we entrust her with *one* single chance to prove that she may do better than she did in the past? And it wouldn't even have to be you who gives her that chance! You'll just have to allow me to do so myself. Just give me permission to give her one lesson with our car. Please. Only one lesson to see how it goes."

His eyes widened and the coldness turned into fear.

"*You* want to do it? So I am supposed to endanger the life of my only son for the sake of such a freak? What if something happens to you? How could I ever forgive myself?!?"

"Nothing's going to happen to me. I'll be fine and Ruth will be, too. Just give us a chance to prove it to you."

"Oh, it is 'us' now, is it?"

"Come on, dad. Please. One chance."

I felt like I was a little boy again and pleaded with him over some new toy I wanted to have.

It's time that I move out of here. Otherwise he'll never stop to see me as his young child …

"George, be reasonable …"

"No, dad, you be reasonable! I'm a grown-up person and I have decided to give Ruth a chance. I would do so on my own, but it's your driving school and your car. So please just give me the permission to use it and I'll do the rest on my own. I'll even take full responsibility if the other driving schools should turn against us."

"They'll hate us, I can tell you that!"

"Maybe. But it's for a good cause."

"Is it? To me it rather looks like a lost cause. This girl isn't safe. She could be freaking out anytime and what happens then?"

"I'll prevent her from damaging anybody, including herself."

"Her last driving instructor wasn't able to stop her!"

"For god's sake, they were driving at high speed! But I won't be. It will be a normal lesson, just around the city and we won't even reach 100 kilometres per hour. All right?"

"Nothing's right. You are completely out of your mind."

"Dad, just drop it. I will do this and there's nothing you can do about it. If you won't give me the car, I will buy one myself and …"

"Now you've lost it! You'll buy a car for that lunatic? Just so that she can lose some of her memories or what? She has committed a murder, George! She is dangerous!"

"No, she isn't. It was the fault of her brain, which is now healthy and well working."

"How do you know?"

"Because her doctors say so and I have talked to her myself. She sounded very normal."

"They always do. And then they stab you in the back."

"This is nonsense, dad. Nobody is going to stab anyone. So please just give me the permission, all right?"

I could see in his blue eyes that his defence was breaking apart and finally – after two days of heated discussions – he gave in.

"All right. If you're going to do it anyway, then you might as well take our car."

"Thanks, dad."

I couldn't keep myself from revealing the relief and happiness and gave him a tight hug – something I normally saved for birthdays and Christmas.

"And when will you be starting?"

"I don't know yet. We'll meet tomorrow and then we shall discuss the whole thing. Maybe Charlotte could draw up some kind of special contract or something."

We spent the rest of the evening talking over certain terms of such an agreement and I went to bed with a head filled with 'But only …' and 'You'll have to …' conditions.

Charlotte wasn't pleased at all to hear about my change of mind and instantly tried to talk me out of it. But when I wouldn't give in and even father told her that it was my choice and responsibility, she finally stopped complaining.

We had just finished to work out a special contract for Ruth when she and her mother arrived at our office. As I told them about our victory, Emilia nearly started crying and wouldn't stop thanking me, while Ruth showed me a smile of real happiness.

"Ruth will be having a few theory lessons first, just so that she remembers the most important things and when the TÜV has approved her, we will start with the driving lessons."

"Thank you so much, Mr. Vogel."

"Please, call me George. Otherwise I will get confused that you might be talking to my father."

Emilia laughed with pure relief and nobody seemed to notice that even Ruth chuckled a little, before the blank face appeared again. When our eyes met, I could see that she knew I had noticed it and she quickly looked away, like she was embarrassed to have shown so much emotion.

"There will be a first bill for the TÜV as soon as you can present us with the results of her eyesight test and the evidence that she has completed a first aid course."

"Oh, I already have those documents with me, if you'd like to see them now."

Emilia quickly opened her handbag and produced all the needed paperwork – which Charlotte took with a false smile and looked them through like she was searching for the slightest chance to get rid of Ruth. When she found nothing wrong, she just nodded and turned towards her computer to prepare the first bill.

"Would you like to pay it now?" she asked coldly and eyed Emilia in a way that clearly stated mistrust of her daughter.

"Yes, of course."

I had to force back my laughter while Charlotte received the money with the face of a stone gargoyle. Finally everything was settled and we arranged a meeting for next Tuesday where Ruth would visit our theory class and have a quick chat with me about the fundamentals of driving. She had passed her last theory test with zero mistakes and so would soon be able to start with the practical part.

After a few more thank you's from Emilia, the two women left our office smiling and Charlotte even put up a friendly face until they had reached their car.

"Gosh, I can't believe it."

Her fake smile dropped instantly and she didn't hold back to express her anger. I listened calmly and nodded occasionally, until the storm was over.

"Well, I'll leave you in charge then," I said when I stood up and left with a soothing smile.

She just grunted and turned towards her computer without so much as looking at me again.

Between heaven and hell

At first her mother had visited her every day, but after a few months the visits slowly ceased and after a year she was only stopping by on weekends – depending on the workload she had to cope with. Without her mother around, it was even more difficult to concentrate on staying sane and not to lose track of what was real and what was a lie.

When she wasn't able to keep up with her stories about aliens anymore, she decided that it was time to show some improvement in the sessions with her psychiatrist. She started to reduce the faked seizures and finally her doctors said that her brain was healing again.

It was at this time that her conscience decided to take over and tormented her with dreams of car crashes and corpses who attacked her in her sleep. She had lots of difficulties to find some sleep at all, but she didn't give up on her mission. She would atone for her sins, yes, but she wouldn't spend the rest of her life in this madhouse. There was still a chance that she might get a normal life again and so she fought to stay sane and carry on.

When she woke up from her nightmares, she always lay in the darkness for a few hours, panting and trying to understand the meaning of her fantasies. She pondered a lot over the question of guilt and responsibility, mostly coming to the conclusion that she had saved the world from the evil of her driving instructor.

But there was also regret for what she had done. She actually started to wonder, if there might have been another way – one without killing and hurting others.

Especially hurting her mother and the innocent driving examiner had been wrong and she spent many tears on the thought of the pain she had caused.

After a while she even mentioned this in her sessions and her psychiatrist said that they were starting to make real progress. The prospect of getting away from all the other lunatics – including the nurses and doctors – was one of the big hopes that kept her going. This and seeing the smiling face of her mother once more.

It still took a few years – she had lost count after one and a half – until the doctors agreed that she was nearly ready to be let out of her maddening prison. In one of the last sessions, her psychiatrist mentioned the advice that it might be helpful for her full recovery if she could continue her driving lessons, once she had gotten used to a normal life again.

There was a lot of paperwork and tests before all of her doctors approved this idea. When she was released from the madhouse to live with her mother again, she still had to visit a psychiatrist for over a year until finally everyone agreed that she was healed and could be trusted with guided driving.

That day her mother told her that they were going to move into a new home, so that they might get a whole new life and a chance to live in peace, without the horrors of the past creeping back to them around well-known street corners.

So they decided to move into a little village in the north of Germany where they hopefully would get a chance to start all over again – or so they thought …

Dawn of hope

Tuesday evening arrived with a lot of tension in the air: Charlotte was still mad at me for 'betraying' her while my father was quite nervous if anybody would recognise Ruth and tell one of the other driving schools about her. His worst nightmare was that somebody might find out that we had accepted her at our school and that we would be regarded as traitors from now on.

I on the other hand was really looking forward to this and hoped that Ruth would have no problems getting into contact with this part of her past. When she arrived punctually at our doorstep and greeted me with half a smile, I was actually quite relieved that she didn't seem to have any trouble with dealing with her memories of driving school. She even tried to smile at Charlotte, but that was a lost cause and she soon seemed to notice. While Charlotte continued to stare at her computer screen with the utmost concentration, I stood up and walked into the little office to greet Ruth with a returning smile.

"Good evening, Ruth."

"Good evening."

I showed her the place where she could hang up her jacket and led the way into the room for theory classes. My father was already there, as were a few early people. They all just stared at their questionnaires and nobody looked up to notice the new girl which took a place right at the back of class. I explained in a hushed voice that she wouldn't have to visit all of the lessons, even though she would have to pass another theory test. But for now she

52

should just try to fill out a few questionnaires, so that we could see if she remembered everything correctly. Ruth nodded and went up to the front to get the paperwork, while I decided to sit in on the class, too. So I found myself a seat not far away from Ruth and watched her standing at my father's desk. He didn't look at her once, just picked a few random questionnaires and handed them to her. I couldn't see her face, but imagined that it perfectly matched the expressionless mask of my father. When she sat down, she gave me a quick side-glance before she started to concentrate on the questions. At first, she really took her time, reading them twice and thinking about the answer, but after a while she picked up the speed, until she was scanning the pages so fast that even I would have had difficulties to keep up. The theory class hadn't even started yet when she had finished all of her four questionnaires and she looked at me enquiring.

"Just hand them over, I'll look them through while you listen to the lesson."

"Thank you."

She handed me paper and pen and turned her concentration to the front, where my father had watched her confused and now hurriedly turned to face the whole class.

"Good evening everyone. Please put away your questionnaires, you will have time to finish them at the end of class."

Everybody turned their eyes up front while I looked through Ruth's paperwork. At first, I held the pen at the ready to correct any mistake she might have made, but then I just put it away and looked them through without having to tag anything. All the answers were correct, even the ones on the last page which she had barely looked upon.

When I was finished searching for flaws, I just watched her from the corner of my eye and tried to understand the way of her mind. *How is it possible for such an intelligent brain to end up fantasising about alien attacks? She must have been really bored if her head thought it necessary to come up with such gimmickry … But at least her intelligence doesn't seem to have suffered too much in all those years she spent in the madhouse. Maybe it was her intellect that finally helped her to snap out of the insanity again …*

At the end of theory class, everybody left the room and I handed back Ruth's questionnaires with an approving smile.

"No mistakes. Pretty good considering the speed with which you read those questions. Did you have any difficulties at all?"

"No."

"I thought so. And do you have any questions concerning anything about the lesson of today?"

"No. It was all pretty clear and well explained."

"I see. All right. I think you are ready for the practical part already, but we'll have to wait for the response of the TÜV. I will tell Charlotte that she can register you for the theory test. So would you like to come back on Thursday for another theory class? I hope that I'll be able to tell you the date of our first driving lesson by then."

"Yes, of course. Same time?"

"Yap."

"All right. I'll be there."

"Great. See you on Thursday then."

"Yes, see you. And have a nice evening, George."

"Thanks, you too, Ruth."

"Thank you."

She stood up with a faint smile and quickly went out of the room to join her mother, who had just arrived at the office door. I could hear them greeting each other with joy and Emilia hugged her daughter all the way back to the car. *Guess I was right about this being a good cause! And even father won't have anything to say against her! She was perfectly polite, paid attention, understood everything and filled out those questionnaires like it was a piece of cake! Ha! I wonder what Charlotte will say about this?*

I went up front with a grin of victory and told father and Charlotte about the flawless paperwork Ruth had absolved. They both didn't quite agree with my happiness, but at least they weren't able to find something to complain about anymore.

I took it as a good sign and drove home with a feeling of real achievement and triumph, already looking forward to my next meeting with Ruth. It might actually have been the first time in my life that I wished for time to speed up so that the next week might arrive with good news from the TÜV and nothing else standing in the way of our first driving lesson.

Second chance

It was the first time since she had moved into this new town that she actually started to feel at home. Up to now everybody who knew who she was had eyed her with fear or hatred and only her mother kept her from losing hope. But now a new ray of hope had arrived in her life and his name was George. He was the first person who didn't seem to despise her for her crimes – it seemed like he really wanted to give her a chance to find forgiveness.

The joy in her mother's eyes when George had told them about his acceptance had been an even greater gift and she was very happy to see her smile. But it had come to her as quite a surprise that she herself had started to smile again – not just forcing her lips to move upwards, but really experiencing something like happiness. In the madhouse, she had never smiled and even leaving it, her face mostly kept on the mask of wax that she had trained so hard to wear. It protected her from the judgement of others and kept her emotions hidden, so that nobody would ever find out about her true feelings.

There actually hadn't been many feelings in her heart since the car crash, mostly emptiness and sometimes fear or fury. But now there was joy. She had even started to laugh again – something that she had thought to be impossible.

This George really seemed to be a nice guy and if he was able to help her, she might really start to forget all the cruelties of the past.

Tuesday had been a very good day for her and her mother and so the rest of the week passed by in a daze of cheerfulness. When Monday finally arrived she even found herself awaiting the next evening with something like pleasant anticipation and was greeted in the driving school by George's welcoming smile. It was very easy to forget her mask around him and she always found herself smiling back at him, before she remembered to keep her feelings in check. The lesson itself was quite dull and she had finished even six of the questionnaires this time. When George gave them back to her after class and told her that there hadn't been any mistakes, she really dared to hope that her life might start to be joyful from now on.

This hope was encouraged as George told her and her mother that the TÜV had approved all her paperwork and that she would be able to take her theory test on Friday. If it went well, she would be able to take her first driving lesson whenever she wanted.

Her head couldn't believe her luck at first, but then she gladly accepted his proposal to start as soon as possible. After a quick glance into the schedule book, Charlotte told them that there would be a free lesson just the next Monday and they agreed to meet at 10 o'clock in front of the driving school.

After wishing them a good evening, George showed them outside and took off himself with a fancy motorcycle. She saw the wary look on her mother's face and quickly stopped admiring the nice machine. But as she lay in her bed that night, she couldn't help thinking about driving a bike herself – just flashing through the woods, the speed and wind lashing around her head, forcing all the bad thoughts and memories to fade away, until nothing was left except pure life itself.

How to be a saviour

Monday proved to be a good day from the start. I woke up to witness a beautiful sunrise and went down to breakfast in an exceptional mood. My father wasn't quite a bundle of happiness like me, but at least he didn't start another argument about my safety and so we shared the meal in peaceful silence. We had done so quite a few times since Ruth had passed the theory test with flying colours. *I will never forget the look on his face when I told him that she only took ten minutes to complete the test!*

When I reached the driving school at half past nine, Charlotte greeted me with a forgiving smile and wished me good luck for the ride. I thanked her and prepared the car, until at five minutes to 10 o'clock Ruth and her mother arrived on our courtyard. Ruth seemed to be perfectly fine and at ease with the upcoming task. Her mother wished me a good day and hugged her daughter one last time before she finally let go and drove away to leave the rest to us.

"Good day, Ruth. How are you feeling today?"

"I'm fine, thanks. And you?"

"Fine, too. Did you celebrate passing the test?"

"A little. It wasn't much of a feast or anything. But mother cooked my favourite meal."

"Very nice. What was it?"

"Vegetable lasagne."

"Sounds good."

"Yes, it was quite tasty. Shall we start then?"

"When you're ready ..."

"Whenever you are."

I gave her an encouraging smile and we both got into the car. I sat on the passenger seat and watched her, while she adjusted the seat, mirrors and seatbelt – without needing any help or giving me as much as one questioning look.

"Well, it looks like you haven't forgotten about the essentials. I guess you may start the car then, so that we can see how you perform with a moving vehicle."

She nodded and turned on the engine with a concentrated look into the mirrors. After checking that the path was clear, we smoothly moved onto the road and started to pick up some speed, until we had reached the speed limit of exactly 50 kilometres per hour. She didn't seem to have any difficulties with the traffic and moved through the streets like it was the easiest thing to do. I only had to give her directions and otherwise watched her closely for any signs of discomfort or lack of judgement.

She didn't show any of those and kept her concentration on the street and surroundings like a professional driver. I remembered what my father had told me about the driving examiner, who had stated in an interview that he would have sworn that Ruth would pass the test with ease until suddenly the accident occurred.

Just like then, Ruth seemed to be in perfect control of the car right now and I couldn't help thinking that she actually had quite a talent for driving. The hour went by smoothly and without any problems – at least none that I could notice. Her face was completely expressionless while she was driving and I couldn't make out what she might be thinking. But from what I observed, there didn't seem to be any issues on her side.

When we eventually came back to the driving school and had parked into the parking lot on the courtyard with exceptional ease, she turned off the engine and looked at me with the questioning look of somebody who awaits his sentence.

"Well … This was pretty good. Especially considering the long break that you've had. I couldn't notice any problems or difficulties. Did you?"

"No, none at all."

"I thought so. You probably have some questions?"

"About what?"

"I don't know. Any situation that occurred on our way. A street sign or anything like that. Or driving in general."

"I don't think so. I had taken quite a few lessons before the accident, so the only thing I might lack is practice."

The calmness with which she spoke of her car crash surprised and encouraged me, that this whole driving thing was really helping her.

"Well, if it's about practice, I might be able to help you out. We could arrange another driving lesson for tomorrow if you want to. I think there was a free spot around 2 pm – we'll better ask Charlotte about it."

"Yes, that would be wonderful."

"All right then."

We were about to get out of the car when she turned back to me again and looked at me with furrowed brows – something I had never seen her do before.

"George? May I ask you a different question?"

"Yes, of course."

I sat back down and smiled at her encouragingly.

"Do you think it will be possible for me to get a driver's license?"

I had expected a question like this, but rather from her mother than from Ruth herself.

"Well … Actually, I don't really know. The TÜV approved your driving lessons, but they didn't state if you would be allowed to do another driving examination. If you want to, I could call them tomorrow morning …"

"That would be great. Thank you very much."

"You're welcome."

We smiled at each other for a second until she hurriedly looked away and started to get out of the car. I followed her quickly and we went into the office to arrange our next driving lesson with Charlotte. I had been right about the free hour and so we agreed to meet at 2 pm the next day. As Ruth went out to greet her smiling mother with a warm hug, I turned to Charlotte and gave her a confident 'I told you so'-look.

"Yes, all right. You survived. Congratulations."

"Thank you so much Charlotte, I really appreciate your defeat."

"Ha! We shall see about that! There are still some lessons to come."

"Yes, yes. Is father still here?"

"No, he has gone home to prepare lunch."

"All right. I'll better join him to assure him of my safety, too."

"I bet he'll be relieved."

"Sounds like I have been away in a war."

"Almost."

I rolled my eyes and wished her a good day before I went home to my father and found him already waiting in eager anticipation. When I entered the house, he dashed to the door and hugged me with a sigh of relief — something he hadn't done for many years.

"It's all right, dad. I'm fine."

"Thank god! I really wasn't sure … But now it's over. How was it? Any difficulties?"

"None at all. She seemed to be very comfortable with driving and I only had to tell her where to go. It was quite impressive actually."

"I see. Well … I guess her doctors were right then. Will you be driving with her again?"

"Yes, tomorrow."

"Oh. Already?"

"Dad, it's going to be fine. She can handle it."

"If you say so."

He continued to question every detail of our tour while we had lunch together and I was quite relieved when he had to get back to the driving school himself.

While he was away, I spent a few hours researching Ruth's case on the internet, but I couldn't find anything on her former driving examiner. When I was finished, it was already about six o'clock and so I went into the kitchen to prepare dinner.

Dreams and nightmares

She lay awake and stared into the darkness but not really seeing it. Instead her vision was clouded by flashes of memories which kept her mind too busy to find its way to sleep.

It had been quite a while since she had had her last nightmare about the car crash and she had hoped that this part of her past might be forgotten at long last. But todays driving lesson had brought back some memories she would have rather buried than relived once more.

A picture of blood, flesh and cracked bones flashed through the night and made her gasp. Would the past be haunting her for the rest of her life? Was this the path of redemption or had she probably become insane after all?

With an exhausted sigh, she turned to her right side and closed her eyes in an attempt to get rid of all those thoughts and visions. But they kept following her whenever she tried to escape them and would have followed her into her dreams if she would have been able to fall asleep – which wasn't the case.

After two hours of silent torment, she finally gave up and turned on the light. The brightness drove away the darkness in her mind, but the feeling of guilt remained. She took the notebook from her bedside table, opened a blank page and started to draw without really planning it. Her hand just kept flying over the paper until the outlines of a face showed up. The pencil kept adding details and she started to recognise the person that her unconsciousness had come up with: George.

A smile found its way onto her face and she finished the drawing with a feeling of warmth and confidence. George believed in her – she had felt it while they were driving through the city together. He would be the key, the one to open up the doorway towards a new future, bright and shining, so that the dark past might turn into nothingness and finally be forgotten.

The hero of everyday life

I woke up early and had breakfast before my father even got up – which was very unusual. But it gave me some time to enjoy the peacefulness and silence until his worries would unload themselves upon me once more.

When I had cleaned the dishes, I remembered that I had promised Ruth to check if she would be able to get a driving license and just had picked up the phone when my father entered the living room.

"Awake already?"

His voice didn't indicate any special concerns – he was probably trying to sound casual.

"Yes, the sun woke me up."

We both knew that this was a lie, but he just nodded and went into the kitchen while I phoned the TÜV and asked permission to have Ruth examined for a license once more. The bored voice of the woman at the other end of the phone told me that she would pass on my request and give me a call as soon as she had an answer. I thanked her and wanted to wish her a lovely day, but she had already hung up. *It was nice to speak to you, too.*

With a quick glance at the clock, I confirmed that it was time to get to work and so I wished my father a nice day, avoiding any conversation about the upcoming driving lesson. The ride on the motorcycle was finally able to convince my whole body that it was time to wake up and when I reached the bookstore, I felt windblown and freed from all trouble. *Ruth should maybe try this out – it would probably free her mind as well …*

My shift started at eight o'clock and passed by without any complications. I had already told my boss that I would be giving a few more lessons than usual and he agreed to take over the later shifts so that I could leave at noon and get some lunch. Father wasn't home and so I prepared my meal in peace before I set off again and drove to the driving school.

Charlotte greeted me with a cheerful smile and it seemed that she had finally forgiven me my treacherous actions.

"A beautiful day, isn't it?"

She looked at the blue sky which was only frequented by a few little clouds and otherwise presented us with warm rays of sunlight.

"Yes, a nice day indeed."

I returned her smile and had a little chat before I went to get the car keys. Father was just getting back from a driving lesson himself and we switched places without as much as a short conversation.

A few minutes later, Ruth and her mother turned up and I noticed that they both seemed to be in a very good mood. *Just like Charlotte – probably women have a special liking for sunny days …* After a brief greeting, Emilia wished us a nice day and drove off, so that Ruth and I could finally get into the car.

She immediately started to prepare herself for the ride and didn't seem to have any questions about yesterday whatsoever.

"Nice weather today. The sun should be still high enough not to get in our way, but just in case: Do you know how to use the sun visor?"

"Yes."

"Good. Well, we may take off whenever you're ready."

She just nodded and turned on the engine. For the rest of the hour I watched her movements with content and only told her where to go, without having to interfere otherwise. She seemed to be as much at ease as I was and at the end of the lesson I even dared to start a conversation.

"I phoned the TÜV this morning about your driving license. They will be giving me a call within the next few days, but if you want we may still continue the lessons anyway."

Ruth kept her eyes on the street, but I could see the joy enlightening her face.

"Thank you very much. I would really appreciate that."

"Very well. Would you like to check for another lesson this week? I think Charlotte said something about some free hours on Friday …"

"Yes, that would be great."

We smiled in unison and for a few moments I forgot about her craziness and everyone else's concerns – at least until we reached the driving school. All questions and doubtful thoughts returned though as we entered the office and arranged the next lesson with Charlotte.

She didn't show her disagreement of course, but I could feel that she was being quite reserved and not really approving this continuity of my frequent lessons. I tried to ignore this feeling and we agreed on another meeting on Friday afternoon, before Ruth was picked up by her joyful mother and bid us goodbye.

As soon as the door was closed, Charlotte unloaded all her anxiety upon me.

"I really hope that you know what you're doing! The other driving schools will notice it if you keep driving around with her every day. And three lessons within the first week isn't exactly the kind of start I would recommend for such a person."

I had still been watching Ruth getting into her mother's car and now turned to face Charlottes worried face.

"So what is it that you would recommend then? And for whom anyway? Am I the 'such a person'? Do you think I should be taking it slowly, because I normally only give driving lessons every few weeks?"

Her brows met with the utmost concern and formed a stern battle line to conquer my sarcasm.

"You know very well whom and what I meant. This is a serious matter, you know. It might be better if you would give all of us some time instead of this hastiness. What's the rush anyway? Are you trying to set a record or something?"

"Nonsense. She would still have to complete the standard amount of lessons anyway and I don't even know if she will be able to get a license."

"You are planning to have her examined?! Do you really think that there is a driving examiner that would take that risk?"

"Oh please! Would you quit acting like she might kill us all? It was an accident, for Christ's sake! And the driving examiner even survived, so what's the deal?"

"What's the deal? Seriously? She *killed* somebody! Her driving instructor died in that car crash, that's the deal."

"I'm not going to die, alright? She will be fine, she's really good at driving and there are no signs for any relapse."

"Oh, so you're an expert in that matter? Did you study her brain or what?"

"Charlotte, come on! This is stupid ..."

"No, you're stupid if you believe that anyone but you will ever trust her! The TÜV won't allow it, I'm sure and even if they would, you'd have to find a driving examiner insane enough to get into the car with her."

"Fine. I'm stupid then. At least I don't have to live with the knowledge that I turned down somebody who is perfectly trustworthy and deserves a second chance!"

I handed over the car keys without another word and walked out of the door before she could make me feel bad for my rudeness.

Searching for forgiveness

The night after her second driving lesson hadn't been as bad as the first one and she had finally managed to find some sleep. Wednesday however was rather gloomy and brought lots of rain, so she spent the whole day inside and felt kind of trapped after a while.

Drawing was still a good way to escape her thoughts, but when she ended up outlining the scene of the car crash, she hurriedly put away her notebook and just stared into her room. The walls were empty and white – not as bright as the ones in the madhouse, but it still reminded her of the cell and the endless nights of silent tears and screams.

A brief look out of the window confirmed that the weather wasn't about to release her from this prison, so she decided to turn it into something less depressive at least. Her mother was still at work, but she found brush and paint in the cupboard and spent the rest of the day redecorating her room.

At first, she painted the walls with a light blue ground colour and then started adding some ornaments like birds, trees and fluffy clouds. In the end, her whole room looked like it was floating high above the ground and made her feel a bit freer.

The ceiling was still white though, which didn't quite fit the image and so she filled it with a huge sun. The centre of it was of a warm reddish colour which changed into orange on the edges and faded out into bright yellow rays, which entwined with a colourful rainbow.

By the time her mum got home, all the painting utensils were already back in the cupboard and Ruth was lying on her bed, regarding her work with satisfaction.

When her mother entered the room, she stopped dead and eyed the drastic change open-mouthed until a broad smile spread upon her face. Tears of joy started to fill her eyes and she embraced Ruth with such force that it took her by surprise. For a short moment, she lost her composure and felt her eyes getting wet in response to the urge of feelings that was bubbling up inside her.

She put her head against her mother's shoulder and felt the silent tears streaming down her cheeks, leaving little dots on the blouse beneath her face. After a while the first wave of joy was over though and the memory of the last time she had cried overshadowed all the delight she had felt seconds ago. Pictures of the small white cell started to flash before her eyes and she could feel the containment that was starting to lock her feelings away once more.

Her eyes fixed themselves upon the bright colours of her room and she pressed her face into the warmth of her mother's body until the dark thoughts faded away, leaving her empty and longing for oblivion once more.

71

Challenge accepted

"I am very delighted to hear that. Yes … Alright. Thank you very much for your efforts. Yes. Bye."

I put down the phone and grinned at my father with the expression of victory gleaming in my eyes. *Could this Friday get any better?*

"I suppose that you've just spoken to the TÜV …"

My father didn't join my joyful moment and remained as grim as he had been before.

"Yes! I did. And they have accepted."

He snorted and started to turn away.

"Oh, come on. It's not like a death sentence, you know! It's a driving test."

"Yes, with this lunatic and *you* in *my* car. I shouldn't have agreed to all of this in the first place. Maybe I'll just cancel it. I won't allow you …"

"Dad, please. Don't start this discussion now! I've had a wonderful day, Ruth was in a great mood and drove perfectly and the weekend is about to start. Please don't ruin this now."

He eyed me with open disapproval, but didn't continue his argument and just stalked off into the kitchen.

Instantly the smile returned to my face and I had to fight the urge to phone Ruth and tell her about our victory. *Well, it's not really over yet. She will have to finish all the compulsory lessons and I've got to find a driving examiner who is willing to join us for the big day … But still! This is awesome!*

I really didn't know how I was supposed to survive the weekend without telling anybody about this. It was too late to call any driving examiners now and their offices didn't open on a Saturday, so I was facing two days of suppressed delight while being watched by my disapproving father. *Fat chance for a great weekend …*

But I wouldn't let my good spirits be darkened by minor obstacles like this. Instead I went to my room and checked the internet for any useful information about a driving examiner suited for the task.

Dinner passed in silence, because my father wasn't willing to talk about anything cheerful and I was too happy to join his gloom. We both went to bed early and remained silent for most of the weekend.

I couldn't cope with his subtle disapproval all day though and went out on Saturday to meet some friends in the local pub. Even driving my motorcycle felt like a relief already and on my way back home, I took a short detour along the B-road to clear my mind before returning to the dark hole of father's house.

The sun was just about to settle down for the night and filled the sky with her brilliant shades of colour – and then it happened.

Out of nowhere a deer appeared on the street, stopping dead when it entered my front light. I hit the brakes without thinking about it and tried to avoid a collision. The street was lined with trees and my only way to escape a clash was to dodge the deer with a quick swerve to the opposite lane. My brain hadn't registered any other vehicle before and there was no time to think about it anyway. My body acted on pure instinct and I felt myself leaning to one side, avoiding the animal by inches only and switching back to my side of the street. I instantly put the brakes back into action and came to a sudden halt, gasping, adrenalin rushing through my body.

After a split second of shock, I turned my head to look at the deer. It was still standing rooted to the spot and met my gaze with frightened eyes. Then it darted off into the woods and left me to stand on the deserted street, alone and still breathing heavily.

It took a few moments to get my body back under control and I drove home with reduced speed, constantly awaiting another animal to turn up out of the darkness.

Father was already asleep when I reached safety and so I just sat down in the living room and stared into the darkness until the last bit of shock had flowed out of my body.

I might have been dead by now – it wouldn't have taken much. Just a little bit more speed or a wrong turn to the wrong side … I could have crashed into the trees or the deer. Both ways might have resulted in death actually. My imagination was rude enough to present me a few visions of such a lethal accident and I shook my head to get rid of the unwelcome images.

I wonder if Ruth feels this way sometimes – having flash-backs of her car crash and seeing things she'd rather forget. Did she probably feel like this as she was speeding towards the trees? Did her driving instructor feel that way before he died?

I thought about that question for a while until I decided to get ready for bed – not that I felt sleepy, but it wasn't exactly a topic I wanted to ponder on for too long.

My mind seemed to have other plans though and I kept thinking about death while I lay in bed and tried to fall asleep.

Those thoughts kept turning up until Sunday evening, where I finally decided to tell my father about the whole deer-situation, just to get it off my chest. He wasn't pleased of course and kept asking me if I didn't want to stay at home next day.

"I'm fine, dad. Nothing really happened, it was just the shock. But it's over now."

"Are you sure? I mean, you could just take one day off. The bookshop won't fall apart if you … And this Ruth-girl might wait one day longer. She has had three driving lessons last week, that should be enough for …"

"Dad, please. I'm fine. I don't need a break or anything. I just wanted to talk about it."

The look of concern was starting to leave its marks upon his face and I wondered if he would ever smile at me again.

"If you say so," was his final judgement and he dropped the topic.

Nevertheless I was really glad when Monday arrived and I left the house earlier than necessary to drive to the bookshop more slowly than usual. Work kept my mind occupied enough to forget the whole incident and when I finally drove to the driving school, my spirits were back on their peak.

Charlotte wasn't very pleased with the news of the TÜV's approval, but Ruth joined in on my joyful mood and we planned our next few driving lessons in advance so that she would be ready for the examination as soon as I had found a driving examiner.

This task was proving to be a bit more difficult though, because Ruth's reputation preceded her and everybody seemed to assume that she was only waiting for her next chance to crash a car.

We still continued with the lessons however and she had already completed most of them when I finally found an examiner willing to give her a chance.

I told her so after she had finished her night drive with flawless behaviour – even though I had been a bit anxious about the B-road, but that wasn't her fault of course.

She was delighted to hear such good news and we agreed for the examination to take place in three weeks' time, which would give us enough time to finish all the compulsory lessons and practice a little if there should be any particular issues – even though I doubted that she would have any problems at all.

Vestiges of the past

She didn't wake up, because it didn't feel like a nightmare – it wasn't one. It wasn't a dream at all. Just a memory that bore into her sleepy mind and felt so clear and sharp as if she was reliving the moment once more:

It was her first night drive, the one with her former driving instructor. They were gliding through the darkness of the outskirts of their small village and she was getting a bit tired. Her driving instructor was bubbling about his ex-wife as he always did, until he suddenly told her to turn into one of the parking bays of the B-road. She was taken by surprise, but managed to reverse into the parking space without much effort.

Instead of a complimentary remark, her driving instructor padded her on the shoulder and told her to turn off the engine for a moment. She was confused, but followed his order nevertheless and looked at him questioningly.

He just kept smiling and let his hand glide down her shoulder bit by bit until it reached the front of her blouse. Her eyes widened, but otherwise she couldn't move. Her body was frozen in shock and she just felt her heart beating wildly while his sly grin kept her rooted to the spot. His fingers now touched her bra and slid down along her waist until it reached for her skirt.

With a sudden urge of repulsion, she pressed her legs together and tried to remove his hand from her body. His smile wavered for a second and he furrowed his brow with a disapproving look, while his muscles tightened to keep his hand where it was.

"You wouldn't want to ruin your results now, would you?"

The threatening undertone rang in her ears like a death sentence and she knew at once that she didn't stand a chance. There was only this one driving school in their small village and if she rejected him, he would make sure that she would never get a license. Even if she had called the police, there would have been no proof. It was his word against hers and he was the one with power and influence.

His grin widened as he saw the defeat in her eyes and his hand pushed her legs apart with the force of lust. Her mind kept searching for an escape, but she didn't dare to fight him. He was stronger than her and would get his revenge if she told anybody. If anyone would have believed her anyway.

The helplessness made her feel numb. She closed her eyes and embraced this numbness with all her heart to flee from her body while the grabbing hands were demanding their sexual enjoyment.

The aversion finally ripped her out of the memory and she woke up screaming into her cushion while the feeling of the hands on her body felt as real and fresh as if she had been raped once more. Streams of tears were pouring down her face while she tried to get rid of the images of the past.

It was over! He would never touch her again, never touch any of the girls again. She had made sure of that. And one day she would hopefully be able to forget it all …

The final task

The three weeks passed by like days and Ruth seemed to be getting kind of anxious about the driving test. She didn't show it and her driving skills were as good as ever, but she looked a bit tired and tense, so – with only two days to go – I finally decided to mention it to her.

"Are you feeling alright, Ruth?"

She had just turned off the engine and was about to hand over the keys, but stopped dead as she stared at me in confusion.

"Yes, I'm fine. Thanks. Why do you ask?"

"Oh, it's nothing – I mean there is nothing wrong with your driving or anything. It was very good today!"

Relief spread upon her face and she continued to hand over the car keys.

"I just wondered … You've been looking a bit tired lately."

"Yes, I haven't slept so well. But it's going to be fine, don't worry. I won't mess it up after all you've done for me."

"I'm not worried about me, you know." I looked her straight into the eyes and tried to find a hint for anything she was holding back. "I just want for you to feel safe about it. If it should be too much pressure or anything …"

"No, it's fine. Please don't cancel the test! I'm alright."

She suddenly seemed very worried and I regretted to have asked in the first place.

"Fine. I just wanted to make sure … Well, if there is anything that is bothering you … Please feel free to talk to me. About anything. It doesn't have to be a question about the driving. If there is something that … I don't know … Just feel free to talk to me, alright?"

I tried to smile confidently, but she didn't respond. She just stared at me like I had struck her and suddenly I felt an urge of discomfort. The voice of my father rang in my ears, telling me that I should watch my back and be careful not to be her next victim. *Nonsense! She's not going to kill me just because I showed a little bit of concern – that's stupid!*

"Ruth, are you alright?"

My voice seemed to retrieve her back to reality and she looked at me with … *What's that? Longing? Is there really something bothering her and she doesn't know whether to tell me or not? Maybe it wasn't a bad idea after all …*

"Yes, I'm fine." Finally she cracked a smile and looked at me with real gratitude. "I really appreciate your offer, George. But there is nothing to talk about right now. Except …"

She hesitated and stared at her hands. I followed her gaze and noticed for the first time that they were scarred like she had cut herself with a hundred knifes. *Must have taken a bad hit when the car crashed into that tree. I wonder if it still hurts …*

"Why do you believe in me?"

Now it was I who was taken by surprise and froze in my seat.

"I beg your pardon?"

"Why do you believe that I should be allowed to have a second chance? What made you change your mind? I mean, I remember that first day when my mother and I walked into your office. You didn't seem to like or trust me then. What was it that made you reconsider? Why do you trust me now?"

I stared at her for a few seconds, trying to cope with all those questions. *She noticed all of this? Actually, I wouldn't have thought that she noticed anything that day. She seemed so absentminded and …*

It was hard to focus on finding an answer to her question while my mind kept throwing its own questions at me all the while. When I had finally pulled myself together and started to speak again, I did so very slowly and carefully – trying not to hurt her and still being a bit confused as well.

"Everybody should get a second chance if they really deserve it, right? I mean, you seem to have paid for your sins, if you'd like to put it that way. It seemed like you had been punished for you crimes and thus I thought that you might deserve to start all over again."

I looked at her closely and tried to detect any sign of discomfort or disapproval in her face, but she seemed to be even-tempered and stayed very composed.

"So you think I deserve a second chance?"

"Yes, I do."

"And that's why you persuaded everybody else to do so as well?"

"Um … I didn't really … I mean, I wouldn't put it that way …"

"But your father would have rejected me – he did, in fact. And nobody else would have accepted me either. So if you had turned me down, I wouldn't be able to get a license at all. All of this is happening thanks to you."

She smiled at me with real gratitude and I was so astounded that I didn't even notice that I was smiling myself until she started to turn away from me.

"Thank you very much for the conversation and for everything else, George."

"Oh, yes. Sure. You're welcome."

"I will see you tomorrow then."

"Alright. Have a nice day."

"You, too."

I was still sitting in my seat when I heard the car of her mother arriving and hadn't started to move until they were long gone. *What happened just now? I thought that I was the one questioning her about her well-being, but then ... Why did she ask anyway? I mean, how am I supposed to know why I trust her? It's not like I just decided to do so – it happened! That's how emotions work, isn't it?*

I wasn't sure about anything anymore and still my brain came up with a pretty good answer to one of her questions. Because I was very well able to remember the moment where I had decided to give her a chance: It had been that one second when she had looked at me at our first meeting, the moment before she had walked out of the door. Just this one glance had been enough to encourage some part in my heart to believe in her sanity. That pleading look in her eyes had told me that she really longed for forgiveness and somehow I had been chosen by destiny to be the one to give it to her.

Why me? Probably one of the most asked questions in all of human history. But it kept bothering me for the rest of the day, even when I had finally managed to get out of the car.

Sadly, I had nobody to talk to – Charlotte would just snort and roll her eyes at me in a 'you wanted her, now deal with it' sort of manner and father might have been as helpful as calling me 'insane in the first place' – so I pondered on and thought about that matter all on my own.

Thus, it took me quite a while to fall asleep and on Wednesday I was the one looking tired during the driving lesson. Ruth didn't mention it though and seemed to be in a good mood herself, so I told her that she might as well take a day off before her big day. She agreed smilingly and I spent one day in the bookshop, trying to keep me occupied enough so that I wouldn't think about her for one day – which didn't work at all.

My mind couldn't get rid of all its unanswered questions and even in my dreams pictures of Ruth and her scarred hands kept reminding me of all that I didn't know.

Now or never

She hadn't really slept for the last few days, but somehow her body felt wide awake and fully aware of its surroundings. Maybe it was the excitement of the examination or the adrenaline running through her agitated body – anyway her senses were as sharp as they had been on the day of her first driving test.

With the simple difference that she was really planning to get through with this one. Her brain kept telling her constantly that everything was going to be fine and George smiled at her every time she dared to shoot a glance at him.

The driving examiner actually seemed to be as agitated as she felt and she couldn't blame him. She even thought that she had noticed a shaking of his hands when they had been introduced to each other, but now he was just sitting in his seat behind her and calmly giving the directions while they drove to the city.

The reversing into a parking space had been her first challenge and she had mastered it fluently – just like it had been during her first driving test. Since then they had been driving around the city and she was beginning to suspect that the examiner dreaded to get to the motorway.

When he finally announced that they were turning into that direction, she really thought that she detected a certain amount of fear in his voice. Even though she tried to concentrate on the traffic and didn't think about anything his fear might imply.

As they sped down the motorway, she even felt kind of relieved: This time she wouldn't have to kill somebody. She would be allowed to return home and live a normal life. Her mother would be happy again and they would start all over. She would be able to forget the past and move on. She was free.

Relief

"Congratulations, Ms. Kunze."

I could see the joy radiating from Ruth's eyes while the driving examiner shook her hand with an expression of utter relief.

"Thank you very much." She glanced into my direction and then smiled at the examiner.

"It was very brave of you to drive with me, so I should be the one congratulating you."

The poor man was a bit taken aback by this, but when I started to laugh, he finally let go of all his agitation and happily joined in.

"Yes, well … This reputation of yours is definitely utter nonsense. I mean, I don't know what happened to your mind back then, but today you drove perfectly. So, here you go: Your very own, well-earned driver's license."

He handed her the little card and she stared at it with such amazement as if she hadn't believed to ever get a license after all.

Smiling broadly, I now went over to congratulate her myself and she beamed back at me with pure joy. *It really suits her! She should quit all those composed poker faces and show a bit of emotion sometimes. Gives her eyes a nice sparkle.*

When the driving examiner had left and even Charlotte had gotten off her high horse to congratulate Ruth for passing the test, we both went outside to wait for her mother. Standing there on the walkway, we finally had a private moment and it seemed like this had been the opportunity Ruth had been waiting for.

As soon as the door was closed behind us, she turned to me — still a broad smile on her face — and I already knew what was about to happen before she embraced me with all her might.

"Thank you so much, George. I wouldn't have made it without you!"

Her strength surprised me even more than the act of gratitude itself, but I tried not to show any of that and just padded her on the back.

"You're welcome. And you really did a great job, so congrats once more."

She probably wouldn't have let go of me any time soon, but we both heard her mother's car approaching.

Emilia was all happiness of course and might have hugged me as well, but my father arrived at the driving school just then, so she just kept thanking me repeatedly. In the end, the stern look of Charlotte and the cold behaviour of my father made them leave, but not without inviting me to their first drive.

"I thought it might be nice for Ruth if you'd be there. You know, just for the feeling of having somebody with her — somebody other than me."

"Oh, yes. Um … of course. Why not. When were you planning to drive for yourself?"

Ruth looked at her mother with a bit of unease before she turned back to me.

"I don't know. It's probably enough for today — with all the excitement and … Maybe tomorrow? Then I could calm down a little and … Oh, but that would be Saturday! You don't work on weekends, right? So probably we should wait …"

"No, that's fine. It wouldn't be like working at all. More like … being given a lift by a friend."

I could feel her relief when I smiled at her and she gladly returned the smile.

"Alright. If that's fine by you …"

"Absolutely."

Her mother was delighted of course and we agreed on a time where they would pick me up to join Ruth's first driving experience.

After thanking me once again, they finally left and I could already feel the dark clouds approaching as I turned to face my father.

"She passed then."

It was an obvious statement and I could hear in his voice that he didn't want me to reply, so I just nodded and waited for the lecture.

"But that isn't enough for you, is it? No. Why should it be? Why would you care that I'm glad for you to be alive? You have to join her for a ride – in private! How nice of you!"

He glared at me with open disapproval, but I was too cheerful to get mad at him.

"Dad, it's just a short ride. Please don't make this personal. She has passed the test without a single mistake! This was probably the best driving examination I've ever witnessed!"

"As if you had witnessed many of them!"

"Oh, come on. It's supposed to be a day of celebration."

"Why? Because that lunatic may now drive freely? I don't think that's a good thing …"

"She's not a lune! She is perfectly sane and drives better than you!"

Alright, now I was mad after all. *How does he always get me to explode?*

"George, this isn't about me. I just don't want you to risk your life for that ... that ..."

"Her name is Ruth!"

"For this Ruth-girl, then! Why would you want to do that? We don't do things like this – private driving support! This is absurd ..."

"No, this is called an act of kindness and friendship! I know that those aren't familiar with your way of living, but I like to believe in the best of people!"

"She's still a murderer, George."

"She isn't! And she never was – it was an accident."

"How do you know that?"

"How do you know that it wasn't?!"

We glared at each other for a few seconds until I finally decided that I couldn't stand it.

"You know what? I've had enough of this!"

I turned on my heel and stormed off towards my motorcycle.

"But George ... Your clothes ..."

I ignored him and continued to walk towards my bike.

"You can't drive like that! And driving in a bad mood isn't very wise anyway ..."

"Don't tell *me* what's wise! You don't know anything about wisdom if you can't even find enough forgiveness in your heart to accept Ruth as a normal person!"

With those words, I put my helmet on and started the engine. I knew of course that this would have consequences – and that it really wasn't advisable to drive without further protection. My jeans wouldn't be much help in an accident and my shirt surely wasn't going to keep me warm for long either. But I didn't care. I just wanted to get away. So I sped off, feeling the concerned look of my father burning holes into my back until I had turned around the first corner.

The cold air had already cooled down my quick temper by then and I slowed down a little to get back within the speed limit. *This is madness! I haven't driven as foolish as this since … Well, I don't really remember. But father always manages to get me mad enough to act like a teenager again! Totally stupid – why couldn't he just have been glad for Ruth?!*

I tried to get rid of all those irritating thoughts and to concentrate on the traffic instead. It wasn't rush hour yet, so I hadn't much to worry about. But the city still seemed too busy for me and slow driving wasn't exactly what I was looking for either.

So I turned onto the next B-road as soon as possible and sped up until the wind was lashing around me with icy blows. My ears were filled with the sound of the air rushing past and the adrenaline finally flushed all the anger out of my veins.

After that, it didn't take long until I turned around and sped home to reconcile with my father. He wasn't really willing to forgive me, but his relief that I was safe and alive was greater than his anger and so we made our peace with each other.

He still tried to talk me out of joining Ruth for her first drive while we had dinner together, but after a while he let go of the topic and we finished our meal in silence. I appreciated his defeat, but I was a little anxious as well. How would Ruth perform when she was in full charge of the vehicle? There would be no brakes on my side to help her out. Not that I thought she would need it, but I wasn't sure if her mother was going to make her nervous.

Would she be eyeing Ruth from the rear seat like the driving examiner?

I pondered over those questions for a while, but as soon as I went to bed, I noticed far more pressing problems: Like my father had feared, my body hadn't appreciated the ride without protective gear and I must have become hypothermic without noticing it. Maybe my kidneys had suffered the most, because I hadn't been wearing a kidney belt and the cold wind had had easy access through my thin shirt.

Whatever it was, my body felt a bit feverish as I went to bed and soon enough the next morning showed the full extent of my foolishness.

I woke up with a start, because I had dreamed that I crashed into a tree with my motorcycle. But soon I noticed that this wasn't the reason why I felt so sweaty and was shivering when I got up. *Shit! That's really the worst of all days to get a cold!*

My body didn't give a damn about my disapproval though – which was quite fair, because I hadn't given a shit about my health while I was driving without protective gear. The price was higher than I had guessed. I was shivering all over as soon as I left my bed and even a hot shower wasn't able to warm me up.

I didn't want to abandon Ruth on her first driving day though and tried my best to look as normal and healthy as possible as I went down to breakfast – without any luck.

My father seemed to have been sensing my misery before I even turned up and just eyed me with an 'I told you so'-look on his face. The fact that I was wearing a thick hoodie probably gave me away anyway, but otherwise I would have kept shivering and that could have caused even more suspicion.

Luckily, my stomach wasn't affected by the whole affair and eagerly took in the warm tea and two slices of bread. I had just finished the latter when my father finally decided to break the silence and tell me his deduction.

"So you've caught a cold."

I hated it when he stated things in a way that it was clear he didn't expect an answer and thus gave me no opportunity to answer with 'No'.

"I told you that it wouldn't be wise to drive like that."

Another useless statement! Why is he talking at all? I won't even have to be here – he might have stated those things while I was still asleep for all the effect it has …

"I'm fine."

I stared at my empty plate and tried to decide if I should eat another slice.

"You are wearing a jumper in late summer. This is not very like you."

"I'm just feeling a bit cold. And autumn isn't so far away, you know."

"Don't tell me that you still want to drive around with that Ruth-girl?"

"Yes, of course. Why not?"

I decided that I couldn't eat another slice of bread and finally looked up to meet his eyes. The grey concern met me with all his might and I regretted my decision almost instantly.

"If you are not feeling well, you shouldn't be driving around. A day of relaxation might be better for you after all that stress of the driving test and ..."

"There was no stress! It was fine and I'm fine now. No need to worry."

I got up a bit too fast in my hurry to flee from his concerned look and the room started to spin like a roundabout. I had to hold on to the table until everything seemed stable again and went back to my room without looking in my father's direction – I could feel his worried eyes following me anyway.

They were also waiting for me as I came down the stairs once more, but this time the doorbell saved me from another inquisition.

"Good morning, George."

Ruth beamed at me with a sunny smile and soon enough my cold was forgotten. I bid my father goodbye and hurried to the well-known small car, making my head dizzy again in all the rush to get away from home.

"Are you feeling alright?"

Ruth glanced at me with true concern and I noticed that it didn't bother me as much as the worried eyes of my father.

"Yes, I'm fine. Just a little unstable this morning. But the only thing I've got to do now is sitting beside you and enjoying the ride, right?"

She returned my smile and nodded.

"In that case I'm ready to go."

A hint of her beaming smile enlightened her eyes again and we both got into the car, where I was greeted by Emilia with pure joy. It took a few minutes until Ruth and I convinced her that she might stop thanking me for all I had done, so that we finally could get started.

"Do you want me to say anything or shall I just …? I mean, do you have any kind of planned route or something?"

I looked at Ruth – who didn't really seem to be in charge of this whole event – and then at her mother. Emilia returned Ruth's asking look before she turned to me and smiled.

"I think, it would be best to leave it all to Ruth. You said that her performance is flawless and she has my complete trust anyway. Let's just drive through the city or the surroundings. Whatever makes you happy, my dear."

The last words were directed towards Ruth of course, who seemed to be a bit nervous about all those compliments, but tried her best to keep up the smile.

"Alright. No comments then. You may freely choose the direction."

I leaned back and looked at her in a – hopefully – encouraging way.

"Alright. I'll … I'll just improvise then."

Her eyes were still a bit insecure, but she nodded at me and turned towards the steering wheel.

Repentance

George didn't look like he was as sound as a bell, but he still seemed willing to join them for the ride. Her mother was over the moon of course and so – with a final glance into George's direction – Ruth turned the key and started the engine.

In the beginning, it was a bit confusing to sit in her mother's car, but George's presence made it feel like a normal driving lesson and helped to keep her hands calm and steady. Even her mother tried her best not to be too nervous – she just kept babbling about unimportant things like the weather and traffic situation.

When the first few minutes had passed, she could even widen her view and noticed that George was glancing at her from time to time. He had done so in the driving lessons as well, but now it was a different kind of look. While he normally just seemed to check if she was in control of the vehicle, he now seemed to be interested in her as a person.

She couldn't really make out the difference and tried to concentrate on the street signs and traffic lights instead. After half an hour of driving, she finally felt like it was some kind of routine and let go of all the secret doubts that had still been hiding in her mind. The memories of her fatal first driving test seemed to fade into obscurity and there was actual hope that her sins might be forgiven and forgotten one day.

A playful smile danced around her lips and made her eyes sparkle. She would have a normal life again. A life with days of joy and people who actually acted like friends

– maybe even were friends. She wasn't so sure if George would accept that term or felt the same, but her instinct told her that it was there: true friendship and forgiveness.

Alright, there was nothing to forgive in his case, but it still felt like redemption to be driving around with his friendly presence beside her. He had been the first one to give her a second chance, the possibility to start a new life.

Their eyes met when she glanced in his direction once more and his lips answered to her smile like it was the only possible reaction. She could feel her heart beating and turned back to the windscreen with the most curious feeling in her body.

Maybe that was what real happiness felt like. She didn't remember that from her life before the accident, but she was sure that this was something positive, something wholesome – and hopefully the beginning of a better life.